Once there was a little girl named Thala who lived in a town called Kalisz, Poland with her mother and her grandmother.

She had a parakeet named Sigmy that she loved very much. She played with her parakeet and fed him and cleaned his cage.

Thala's mother and grandmother would serve her soup. They served the soup with her favorite silver spoon. The parakeet would love to watch her eat her soup with the spoon all the time.

One day Thala had some friends over her house and she had forgotten to play with Sigmy.

Sigmy felt lonely and decided to go out and make friends of his own. He said, "I will have a new adventure and see the world."

Once the cage was opened, Sigmy flew away to new places. "I can make some more friends by trying to be like them," Sigmy said.

He passed a pond and saw a fish swimming.
Sigmy tried to swim like the fish.

8

Then he got wet and didn't like it.
He shook off the water and went on his way.

Then he met a guard dog that was mean and growly. He tried to be mean like the dog but just made funny sounds and couldn't scare anyone.

After that, he flew to a forest. He met a baby bear and hugged him. "Maybe I can like everyone and then I will have friends," he said.

But the bear got annoyed and ran away.

Then he flew to the park and saw a cat.

Next, he flew to a zoo and saw a monkey scratching
and jumping. Sigmy tried to imitate the monkey
but felt silly doing this.

Afterwards, he flew to a farm and saw a pony pulling a cart.

He tried to pull another cart and got very tired doing so.
He then said, "This is not for me."

Then he flew to a window of a tavern and saw a little girl having soup with a spoon. Seeing this girl stirring her soup reminded him of Thala and how he missed her.

He then flew home and he immediately saw Thala in the kitchen. She was having soup with her favorite spoon.

Sigmy was so happy to be back home with Thala and seeing the spoon made him realize this. "There is no place like home!" Thala and Sigmy were so happy to see each and be together again.

The spoon had a magical meaning to Sigmy because it reminded him of not only being himself but also being at home.

DEDICATION PAGE

This book is dedicated to the spoon that saved Alice Geisinger's mother and grandmother's lives. Her mother, Tola Cymbler and grandmother, Helena Zajdlic, were survivors of the Holocaust in Auschwitz, Poland.

They were on a line to be shot by the Nazis. On the other side, were people stirring a big pot of soup. Alice's mother and grandmother somehow were able to get off the line and start stirring the soup with a spoon. Both of them were forgotten by the Nazis.

After being liberated they managed to save the spoon.

Alice Geisinger has kept the spoon as a memento because it will always have a special meaning for her.

Alice Geisinger was born in Kalisz, Poland after World War II. She lived with her mother and grandmother. Her father died when she was a little baby. She enjoyed eating soup at home.

To order additional copies of this book, contact:
Xlibris
844-714-8691
www.Xlibris.com
Orders@Xlibris.com

ISBN: Softcover   978-1-4691-8488-3
        EBook   978-1-6698-1795-6

Print information available on the last page

Rev. date: 03/25/2022

Printed in the United States
by Baker & Taylor Publisher Services